# Newspaper Capers

## ACTIVITIES TO ACQUAINT STUDENTS WITH NEWSPAPERS
### Grades 4–6

Written by **Michael Lenhart**
Illustrated by **Beverly Armstrong**

# The Learning Works

**Edited by Sherri M. Butterfield**

The purchase of this book entitles the individual teacher to reproduce copies for use in the classroom.

The reproduction of any part for an entire school or school system or for commercial use is strictly prohibited.

No form of this work may be reproduced or transmitted or recorded without written permission from the publisher.

# Contents

**Newspaper Capers**
© 1986—The Learning Works, Inc.

3

# Introduction

The first ten amendments to the U.S. Constitution, which were ratified in 1791 and are known collectively as the Bill of Rights, guarantee freedom of religion, of speech, and of the press to all citizens of the United States. In this country, it is against the law for the federal government to tell newspaper reporters what they can write or to tell newspaper publishers what they can print. As a result, newspaper editors are free to cover and interpret the news as they see fit.

With this freedom comes a responsibility to be honest and to be fair. Newspapers must report the news accurately, interpret it fairly, distinguish clearly between facts and opinions, get the facts straight, and—where appropriate—attribute both facts and opinions to their sources.

Unfortunately, the citizens of some countries do not enjoy the freedoms that are guaranteed to U.S. citizens. Freedom of the press is unheard of in many places. For example, in the Soviet Union, the government strictly controls the information that is published in both books and newspapers. As a result, the truth is often hidden from the people.

**Newspaper Capers** is a self-contained activity unit designed to help you get better acquainted with your local newspaper. As you work on this unit, you will add more than fifty newspaper-related terms to your vocabulary. In addition, you will learn about the people who make the news and the people who report and write about it. When you have finished this unit, you will know how to put your newspaper to work for you to find a bargain, plan a picnic, decide what coat to wear, or sell a toy you have outgrown. And you will understand more fully the importance of freedom of the press.

Illustrations have been added to this book to make it more fun for you to look at and to use. In some instances, these illustrations appear in the boxes and spaces in which you are instructed to paste articles and pictures clipped from your local newspaper. In these instances, you may paste your articles and pictures directly over the illustrations or, if you prefer, you may paste them on the back of the page so that the illustrations remain uncovered.

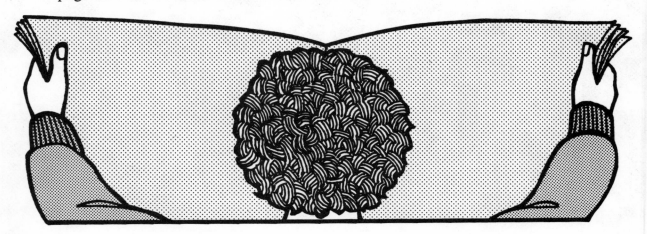

# Grading System

You have an opportunity to choose in advance the grade you will receive on this newspaper unit. Review the various point categories and grade equivalents listed below and then set a goal for yourself.

| Category | Points Possible | Points Earned |
|---|---|---|
| **Complete Notebook**<br>(2 points per page) | 90 | |
| **Bonus Boxes**<br>(1 point each) | 15 | |
| **Vocabulary Words**<br>(3 points for each complete entry) | 39 | |
| **Current Events Presentations**<br>(24 points each for four presentations) | 96 | |
| **Special Projects**<br>(5 points each for six projects) | 30 | |
| **Final Test** | 50 | |
| **Totals** | 320 | |

I would like to earn _____ points and receive a

letter grade of _____ on this unit.

_____  _____
_(signature)_                          _(date)_

**Grade Equivalents**

285-320 points = A
255-284 points = B
225-254 points = C
195-224 points = D

# Pretest/Posttest

Write **T** on the line in front of each statement that is **true**. Write **F** on the line in front of each statement that is **false**. (10 points)

1. _____ A **subscription** is an agreement to take and pay for a newspaper that is delivered regularly.

2. _____ An **insert** is a separate section of a newspaper.

3. _____ The **masthead** is the name of the paper displayed across the top of the front page.

4. _____ A **by-line** is the name of the writer of the story, which usually appears below the headline and above the story in a newspaper.

5. _____ A **lead** is the most important story of the day.

6. _____ A **picture story** is a photograph that illustrates a long news story.

7. _____ **Copy** is typewritten material intended for publication in a newspaper.

8. _____ The **dateline** is the opening word or words of a news story giving the place in which the story originated and, occasionally, the date on which the story was written.

9. _____ In a newspaper, an **illustration** is a hand-drawn picture.

10. _____ A **feature story** is an article whose purpose is to change public opinion by attacking, defending, praising, or teaching.

11. Name the four kinds of news stories. (4 points)

    a. _____    c. _____

    b. _____    d. _____

12. Name the five Ws that are included in the leads of most well-written news stories. (5 points)

    a. _____    c. _____

    b. _____    d. _____

          e. _____

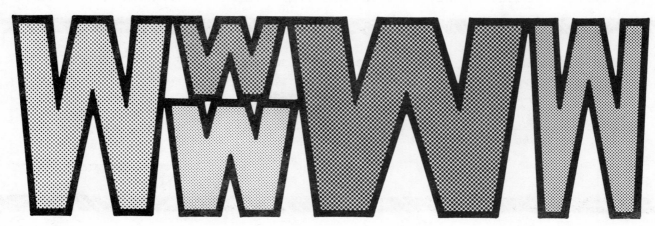

# Pretest/Posttest
## (continued)

Match the following terms with their definitions by writing the correct letter on each line. (18 points)

13. ____ banner

14. ____ beat

15. ____ caption

16. ____ classified ads

17. ____ column

18. ____ columnist

19. ____ edit

20. ____ edition

21. ____ editorial

22. ____ filler

23. ____ flag

24. ____ headline

25. ____ index

26. ____ kill

27. ____ laserphoto

28. ____ standing headline

29. ____ syndicated column

30. ____ tip

A. a piece of advance or confidential information that may lead to a news story

B. words that appear in large type above a story and tell what the story is about

C. a photograph transmitted by a news-gathering or wire service to member or subscribing newspapers

D. a narrow, vertical section of printed words on a newspaper page

E. advertisements that appear together in a single section and are organized, or classified, by type

F. an article expressing the opinion of the newspaper editor and/or owners on a current issue or topic of interest

G. a person who regularly writes an article, or column, for a newspaper

H. a headline in large type that extends across a newspaper page

I. a relatively short and unimportant story or a single fact that is used to fill a column

J. the place or places a reporter goes regularly to obtain news

K. to organize and correct copy so that it conforms to house standards and style

L. a written explanation above or below a photograph or illustration

M. one issue of a newspaper, usually produced in a single press run

N. the name of a newspaper as displayed at the top of the front page

O. a list of the contents of a newspaper, usually found in a box on the front page

P. to stop a story from being published

Q. a headline that is used regularly in a newspaper to identify a column or feature

R. an article or feature that appears regularly in many newspapers across the country

# Pretest/Posttest
## (continued)

Write complete sentences to answer the questions below.

31. Newspapers have an important responsibility to their readers. (4 points)

    a. What is that responsibility? _____

    _____

    b. Why is it important? _____

    _____

32. What are two responsibilities of a news editor? (4 points)

    a. _____

    _____

    b. _____

    _____

33. Why is advertising important to a newspaper? (2 points)

    _____

    _____

34. How do the freedoms guaranteed to citizens of the United States differ from those guaranteed to citizens of the Soviet Union? (3 points)

    _____

    _____

| Scoreboard | | |
|---|---|---|
| Question Numbers | Scores | |
| | Possible | Actual |
| 1-10 | 10 | |
| 11-12 | 9 | |
| 13-30 | 18 | |
| 31-34 | 13 | |
| **Totals** | **50** | |

# Taking Inventory

Circle the number that best represents your response to each statement.

| | Every Day | Sometimes | Never |
|---|---|---|---|
| 1. I check the newspaper quickly to see what TV programs to watch. | 3 | 2 | 1 |
| 2. I enjoy browsing through the newspaper. | 3 | 2 | 1 |
| 3. I use the index to find the specific items that interest me. | 3 | 2 | 1 |
| 4. I enjoy reading the comic section. | 3 | 2 | 1 |
| 5. I notice where news stories originated. | 3 | 2 | 1 |
| 6. I enjoy reading the sports section. | 3 | 2 | 1 |
| 7. I enjoy reading feature stories. | 3 | 2 | 1 |
| 8. I read some of the editorials. | 3 | 2 | 1 |
| 9. I read some of the letters to the editor. | 3 | 2 | 1 |
| 10. I enjoy reading local or syndicated columns. | 3 | 2 | 1 |
| 11. I look at the display ads in the newspaper. | 3 | 2 | 1 |
| 12. I use the newspaper to find out what movies are playing at local theaters. | 3 | 2 | 1 |
| 13. I glance at the business section. | 3 | 2 | 1 |
| 14. I read some of the classified ads. | 3 | 2 | 1 |
| 15. I read the weather report. | 3 | 2 | 1 |

### How Do You Rate?

**35–45**  You are making good use of your newspaper.

**25–34**  You could make better use of your newspaper.

**15–24**  You need to get acquainted with your newspaper.

Column Totals

Total from **Every Day** column _____

Total from **Sometimes** column _____

Total from **Never** column _____

**Total Score** _____

# Building Vocabulary

As you read your local newspaper, you will find some words that are unfamiliar to you. Write these words on the lines below. Look up these words in a dictionary. On the lines beside each word, write the pronunciation key, part of speech, and definition that match the way the word was used in your newspaper.

| Word | Definition |
|------|------------|
| *indict* | *(in-dīt') verb; to charge with a crime* |
| | |
| | |
| | |
| | |
| | |
| | |
| | |
| | |
| | |
| | |
| | |
| | |
| | |
| | |
| | |

# Making a Current Events Presentation

The purpose of giving oral presentations is to practice and develop good communication skills. Following these steps will help you give more effective current events presentations in class.

## Steps to More Effective Current Events Presentations

**1.** Select an interesting newspaper article.

**2.** Read the article carefully. Find out what happened, to whom, when, where, and why.

**3.** Reread the article. As you do so, underline the essential facts and the most important details.

**4.** On an index card or a sheet of paper, summarize the article in your own words. Be sure to include the facts and details you underlined.

**5.** Read the summary to yourself several times so that you become thoroughly familiar with its content and know how to pronounce all of the words.

**6.** Practice giving the summary aloud in front of a mirror. Be aware of your posture and of how frequently you look up at the "audience" and how much you look down at your notes.

**7.** Time the oral presentation of your written summary. If necessary, omit some of the details so that it can be given easily within one to two minutes.

**8.** When you give your presentation in class, stand up straight, look directly at the audience, speak clearly and at a normal pace, and refer to your notes only to confirm important names and numbers.

## Oral Presentation Rating

4 Excellent ☐    3 Good ☐    2 Fair ☐    1 Needs Improvement ☐

| Criteria | Ratings | | | |
|---|---|---|---|---|
| **Article Selection** (interesting, appropriate) | | | | |
| **Posture** (straight but not rigid) | | | | |
| **Eye Contact** | | | | |
| **Clarity** (how easily understood) | | | | |
| **Pace** (neither too fast nor too slow) | | | | |
| **Use of Notes** (for names, numbers only) | | | | |
| **Totals** | | | | |

# The Front Page

---

### Terms to Learn

**flag**          (or **nameplate**) the name of a newspaper as displayed at the top of the front page

**edition**      one issue of a newspaper, usually produced in a single press run

**banner**      a headline in large type that extends across a newspaper page

**column**     a narrow, vertical section of printed words on a newspaper page

**index**       (or **departmental index**) a list of the contents of a newspaper, usually found in a box on the front page

---

Look at the front page of your local newspaper. Find the answers to the following questions and write them on the lines.

1. What is the name of your newspaper? _____

   _____

2. What is the date of your newspaper? _____

3. How many pages are in this particular issue and edition of the paper? _____

4. Many newspapers have more than one section. How many sections are in today's edition of your newspaper?_____

5. What is the cost of today's edition? _____

6. Is there a headline that extends across the top of the front page of your paper? _____ If so, write it here. _____

   _____

7. The banner usually headlines the most important story of the day. In two or three words, write the topic of the most important story. _____

8. How many columns are on today's front page?_____

9. Measure all of these columns with a ruler. Are they the same width? _____ How wide are they? _____

10. Is the index in your paper on the front page? _____ If not, on which page is it? _____

---

**Bonus Box**    What does the word **circulation** mean and what is the circulation of your newspaper?

---

# The Index

Cut out your newspaper's index and paste it in the box at the right. Large newspapers are often divided into **parts,** or **sections.** These parts, or sections, are usually labeled with roman numerals or with capital letters. When you are looking for a specific item or feature in a large newspaper, you will need to know both the part numeral or letter and the page number.

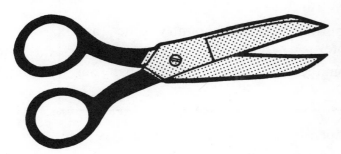

Use this index to locate the items listed below. For each one, indicate the part, or section, and the page.

|   | Part or Section | Page |
|---|---|---|
| 1. Classified Ads | _____ | _____ |
| 2. Comics | _____ | _____ |
| 3. Editorials | _____ | _____ |
| 4. Movies | _____ | _____ |
| 5. Sports | _____ | _____ |
| 6. TV-Radio | _____ | _____ |
| 7. Weather | _____ | _____ |

# EDITORIALS CLASSIFIED ADS MOVIES SPORTS TV&RADIO COMICS WEATHER

**Bonus Box** What are the **obituaries** and where do they appear in your newspaper?

Name _____

# Kinds of News

| | Terms to Learn |
|---|---|
| **dateline** | the first word or words in a news article giving the place in which the story originated and, occasionally, the date on which it was written |
| **local news** | news from your town or city |
| **regional news** | news from the rest of your state (other than your town or city) |
| **national news** | news from the rest of the country (other than your state) |
| **international news** | news from the rest of the world (other than your country) |

Select a brief news story from your paper and paste it in the box on this page. Circle the dateline and answer the questions below.

1. In which city did the story originate?

   _____

2. Would you classify the news contained in this story as local, regional, national, or international?

   _____

3. In five words or less, identify the topic of this story.

   _____
   _____
   _____

**Bonus Box**   Prepare a current events presentation based on this news story. See page 11.

# Kinds of News
## (continued)

Select another news story from your paper and paste it in this box. Circle the dateline and answer the questions below.

BOMBAY SYDNEY LIMA
MONTEVIDEO BRISTOL
BERN GLASGOW ROME
MOSCOW TOKYO OSLO
KHARTOUM SANTIAGO

1. In which city did the story originate? _____

2. Would you classify the news contained in this story as local, regional, national, or international? _____

3. In thirty words or less, summarize the most important facts in this story.

_____

_____

_____

_____

_____

**Bonus Box** Do some research to learn five facts about the city in which this story originated. Write them on the back of this page or on a separate piece of paper.

# Headlines in the News

**Terms to Learn**

| | |
|---|---|
| **headline** | words that appear in large, dark type above a story and tell what the story is about |
| **banked headline** | a headline that contains stacked lines of type of at least two different sizes |
| **standing headline** | a headline that is used regularly in a newspaper to identify a column, feature, or section |

Find an example of each type of headline named below and paste it in the appropriate box.

1. A one-line headline

2. A two-line headline

3. A banked headline

4. A standing headline

# Headlines in the News
## (continued)

5. Find a headline that gives you a clue that the accompanying story is local. Paste the headline in this box. Underline the clue word or words.

6. Find a headline that gives you a clue that the accompanying story is national. Paste the headline in this box. Underline the clue word or words.

Headlines are written to attract a newspaper buyer's attention and to give a newspaper reader some idea about the content of the story that follows. People who write headlines usually use vivid verbs to make them more interesting, eye-catching, or exciting. From your newspaper, select two headlines that you find unusually interesting or exciting. Write them on the lines below. Draw a line under each noun and circle each verb.

_____

_____

_____

_____

 **Bonus Box** Cut out ten news stories of the same column width. Cut off their headlines. Put the headlines in one pile and the stories in another. See how quickly you can rematch the headlines with their stories.

# Who Writes the News?

**Terms to Learn**

| | |
|---|---|
| **Associated Press (AP)** | a cooperative worldwide news-gathering service |
| **United Press International (UPI)** | a worldwide news-gathering service |
| **by-line** | a line at the top of a newspaper or magazine story, just below the headline, which gives the writer's name |
| **filler** | a relatively short and unimportant story or single fact that is used to fill a column |

Men and women called reporters write the news. Individual newspapers cannot afford to have their own reporters in all of the places where news happens. For this reason, they join or subscribe to news-gathering services. The three major news-gathering services are the Associated Press (AP), Reuters, and United Press International (UPI). Stories written by reporters employed by these services are sent all over the world by means of satellites and special telecommunications equipment. Editors read these stories, decide which ones will interest their readers, adjust them to fit the column space that is available, and print them in their newspapers. If a story has been prepared by a news-gathering or wire service, the name of this service appears as a by-line immediately below the headline or its acronym appears in parentheses after the dateline.

Find a story prepared by one of the three news-gathering services. Paste it on the back of this page. Mark and label the headline, the by-line, the dateline, and the name or acronym of the wire service.

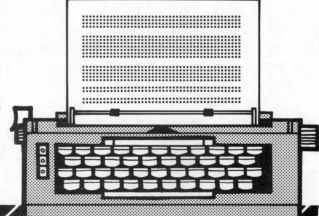

**Bonus Box**  Over a period of a month, collect fillers and paste them on a separate sheet of paper.

# A Look at a Lead

| Terms to Learn | |
|---|---|
| **lead** | the opening paragraph of a news story, which is usually one sentence and no more than thirty words in length |
| **five Ws** | who, what, when, where, and why—the important information that is included in the lead of a well-written news story |

Find and cut out a news story. Paste it on this page. Read the lead of the story to see how many of the five Ws are included. Use this information to answer the questions below.

Who? _____

What? _____

When? _____

Where? _____

Why? _____

# A Look at a Lead
## (continued)

Paste one lead in each of these boxes. Use each lead to answer the questions below the box.

Who? _____
What? _____
_____
When? _____
Where? _____
Why? _____

Who? _____
What? _____
_____
When? _____
Where? _____
Why? _____

Cut out a news story. Cut off the headline and the lead. On the lines below, write a new headline and lead for this story.

_____

_____

_____
_____
_____
_____
_____

**Newspaper Capers**
© 1986—The Learning Works, Inc.                    20

# Pictures in Print

**Terms to Learn**

| | |
|---|---|
| **photograph** | a picture of a person, place, or event taken with a camera and used to tell or illustrate a story or idea |
| **illustration** | a drawing used to tell a story or to clarify an idea |
| **caption** | a written explanation that appears above or below a photograph or illustration |
| **laserphoto** | (or **wirephoto**) a photograph transmitted by a news-gathering or wire service to member or subscribing newspapers |
| **picture story** | an individual photograph or group of photographs used to tell a story with little or no accompanying text |

Photographs and picture stories recreate an event for the newspaper reader and give him or her the feeling of being there. Photographs and illustrations are selected for a variety of reasons, including beauty, emotional appeal, human interest, news value, and unusual effect.

Choose a picture story and paste it on the back of this page. If it has a caption, include it. Reread the reasons for selecting photographs and illustrations which are listed above. Then, on the lines below, tell why you think this photograph or group of photographs was selected to be published in the paper.

_____

_____

_____

# Pictures in Print
## (continued)

First, select an illustration from your newspaper and paste it on this page. Then, on the lines below, tell why you think this illustration was selected to appear in the newspaper.

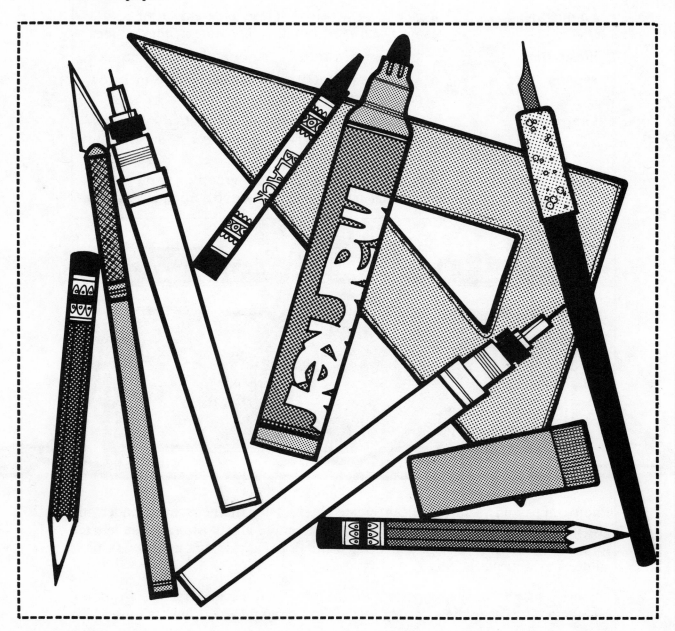

Why was this illustration selected to appear in the newspaper?

_____

_____

_____

# The Inside Story on Reporters

---

### Terms to Learn

**assignment** — a single or continuing story that a reporter is asked to cover for his or her newspaper

**beat** — the place or places a reporter goes or contacts regularly to obtain news, such as school board meetings, the courthouse, or the police department

**deadline** — the time after which copy is not accepted for a particular issue or edition of a newspaper

**tip** — a piece of advance or confidential information which is worth investigating further and may become the basis for a news story

---

Writers hired by newspapers are called **reporters**. It is their job to discover what is happening and to report the news. Some reporters are given special assignments. They are told to find out about a known story or event and to write about it for the newspaper. A few reporters have the same beat every day. They go to the police department, the local hospital, a government office building, or some other place where important things happen regularly and collect information about arrests, accidents, births, deaths, legislation, and the like.

A reporter's job is not easy. Reporters must search out the news, get the facts straight, and spell the names right. To have their stories appear in the paper, they must write them and turn them in before the deadline. Some are hired as staff reporters and are paid a salary; but others, who are called **stringers**, are paid on the basis of the number of column inches their stories fill.

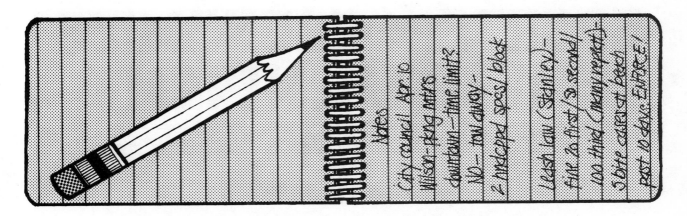

---

**Bonus Box** — Do some research to learn what name is given to a beginning newspaper reporter.

---

# The Inside Story on Reporters
## (continued)

Look through your newspaper to find the names of some reporters. Write these names on the lines below. Beside each name, note the kind of story or stories that reporter wrote. Watch the newspaper every day for two weeks. Each time you see the name of one of the reporters you listed, check to see what kind of story that reporter has written. If the kind is different from what you originally observed and recorded, add it to your previous notation. You will probably discover that some reporters specialize in writing about particular kinds of events while others write about almost anything that happens.

**Reporter**                    **Kinds of Stories He or She Covers**

_____     _____

_____     _____

_____     _____

_____     _____

# HUMAN INTEREST
# SPORTS * ECONOMICS
# ENTERTAINMENT

| **Bonus Box** | From your list above and from your own reading of the newspaper, specify ten kinds of stories and/or types of news in which a reporter might specialize. |
|---|---|

# Meet the Editors

| Terms to Learn | |
| --- | --- |
| **masthead** | the formal listing of a newspaper's name, owners, officers, points of publication, and subscription and advertising rates, which is usually found on the editorial page |
| **editorial** | an article expressing the opinion of the newspaper's editor and/or owners on a current issue or topic of interest |
| **editor in chief** | employee who heads the newspaper's editorial staff, hires other editors and department heads, directs the writing to reflect the policies and wishes of the newspaper's owners, and writes some editorials |
| **news editor** | newspaper employee who examines, edits, and approves all news stories submitted by the various departments |
| **department heads** | persons responsible for the stories written by reporters within various special departments, often including business, government, politics, society, and sports |

Locate the masthead of your newspaper and paste it below. Use it to do the activities on page 26.

# Meet the Editors
## (continued)

Use your newspaper's masthead to complete the following activities.

1. List the names of the officers of the newspaper and their positions.

| Name | Position |
|------|----------|
| _____ | _____ |
| _____ | _____ |
| _____ | _____ |
| _____ | _____ |
| _____ | _____ |
| _____ | _____ |
| _____ | _____ |
| _____ | _____ |

2. List the names of the editors and their specific editorial titles.

| Name | Title |
|------|-------|
| _____ | _____ |
| _____ | _____ |
| _____ | _____ |
| _____ | _____ |

**Bonus Box**    The name of the **publisher** often appears in the masthead. What does the publisher of a newspaper do?

Long before the English word **masthead** was used to name a part of a newspaper, it was used to name a part of some other object. Where would you find this other kind of masthead?

# In the Newsroom

| Terms to Learn | |
|---|---|
| **cover** | to report news about |
| **coverage** | the total amount of news reporting done about any one topic or event |
| **copy** | typewritten material intended for publication in a newspaper |
| **edit** | to organize and correct copy so that it conforms to house standards and style; to direct publication of a newspaper |
| **rewrite** | to revise copy substantially |
| **kill** | to stop a story from being published |

**Word Box**

copy    edition
coverage    headline
deadline    kill
edit    lead
rewrite

First, look at the words in the box. Then, complete this dialogue between a newspaper reporter and a news editor by writing the correct word on each line.

**News Editor:** The [1]_____ in this story is weak. Only two Ws are included in the opening paragraph. I'll have to [2]_____ it before we can print today's [3]_____.

**Reporter:** Can you do it in time to meet the noon [4]_____?

**News Editor:** I hope so. If I can't, I'll have to [5]_____ the story because it's not up to our standards.

**Reporter:** That would be a shame. Without this story, our [6]_____ of that event really isn't adequate.

**News Editor:** Okay! Take it back to your desk, phone Charlotte for some more information, [7]_____ that first part to put some life into it, and have it back on my desk in an hour!

# Editorials

| Terms to Learn | |
|---|---|
| **fact** | a statement that has been or can be proved to be true |
| **opinion** | a statement that is believed but cannot be proved |

The English word **fact** comes from the Latin word *factum*, which means "that which is done; a deed, act, or achievement." A fact is a deed, an act, or something that has been done. It is also a statement about something that actually happened or really exists. A fact is a statement that has been or can be proved to be true.

The word fact has no antonym. No one word is exactly opposite to it in meaning. Several words name contrasting concepts. For example, fiction is not fact, and opinion is not fact. **Opinions** are statements based on feelings or beliefs. They express attitudes, conclusions, evaluations, and judgments.

Well-written news stories contain only facts about an event. They do not include the reporter's attitudes, conclusions, evaluations, and judgments about the event. If statements of this type are included in a well-written news story, they are placed within quotation marks and are attributed to the person who said them, to a source or authority.

In a newspaper, the place for opinions is on the editorial page. There, the editor of the newspaper expresses his or his boss's ideas and opinions about certain topics and current events in special articles called **editorials**.

The purpose of an editorial is to persuade the reader to accept an idea, share an opinion, and/or to take appropriate action. To make the newspaper's readers share its owner's point of view, the editorial writer attacks, defends, praises, or teaches.

# Editorials
## (continued)

**Adjectives** are words used to describe nouns. We use adjectives like *best* and *worst, right* and *wrong* to express our opinions, to say what we think, to indicate that a place is *beautiful*, that a person is *qualified* to hold office, or that a sports activity is *strenuous* or *healthful*. For this reason, an editorial usually contains more adjectives than a well-written news story.

Look through your newspaper to find a news article and an editorial of similar length about the same or closely related topics. For example, they might both be about defense spending, education, fire safety, health, physical fitness, traffic problems, or an upcoming election. Cut out both articles and paste them on the back of page 28. Circle the adjectives used in each one. Underline the opinions expressed in each one. Count the number of adjectives used, the number of opinions expressed, and the total number of words in each article. Enter these numbers in the correct columns of the table below.

|  | News Story | Editorial |
|---|---|---|
| **Number of Adjectives** |  |  |
| **Number of Opinions** |  |  |
| **Total Number of Words** |  |  |

Compare these numbers. In which article were more adjectives used?_____

_____

In which article were more opinions expressed? _____

What is the opinion of the writer of the editorial? Write one sentence summarizing it on the lines below.

_____

_____

What is the opinion of the news reporter? Summarize it in a single sentence on the lines below.

_____

_____

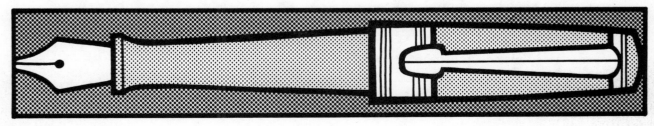

# Letters to the Editor

Newspaper readers express their opinions by writing letters to the editor. Most newspapers have a special page or section in which these letters are published and, in some instances, responded to. Find this section in your newspaper, cut out one letter, and paste it on this page. Then answer the questions below.

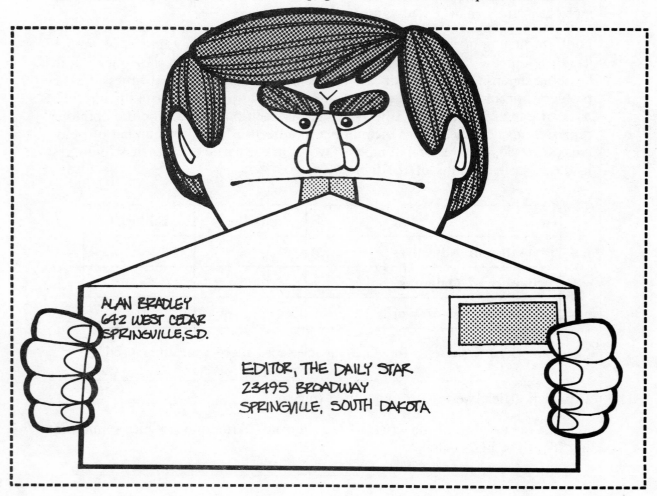

1. Does the letters-to-the-editor section of your newspaper have a special name or title? _____ If so, what is it? _____

2. In five words or less, name the topic of this letter.

_____

3. In a single sentence, summarize the opinion of its writer.

_____

_____

_____

# Feature Stories

**Feature stories** are distinctive newspaper articles that are written to educate and to entertain. Feature stories may be about a variety of topics, including archaeology, celebrities, family life, or travel. They may contain both facts and opinions. Select a feature story and paste it on this page. Then answer the questions below.

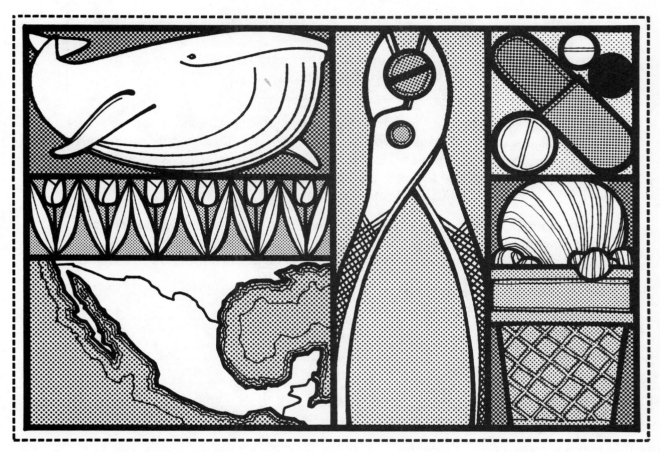

What is the subject of this feature?

_____

Was it written primarily to educate or to entertain?

_____

Underline the main ideas expressed in this feature and summarize them on the lines below.

_____

_____

_____

_____

_____

# Columns and Columnists

---

**Terms to Learn**

| | |
|---|---|
| **column** | a newspaper feature that is written regularly by one writer, usually under a by-line |
| **columnist** | a person who regularly writes a special column for a newspaper |
| **syndicated column** | a column that appears regularly in many newspapers across the country |

---

The English word **column** has more than one meaning. A column can be a narrow, vertical section of printed words on a newspaper page. A column can also be a special feature that appears in a newspaper on a regular basis. Columns are written about a variety of topics, including business, dating, general advice, health, marriage, medicine, politics, sports, and travel.

Some columns appear only in local newspapers. Other columns are **syndicated**, which means that they are purchased from the people who write them and are then sold for regular publication in a number of newspapers throughout the country.

Watch your newspaper for the next two weeks for local and syndicated columns. Summarize what you learn on the lines below.

**Column Title:** _____

**Name of Columnist:** _____

**Column Topic:** _____

_____

**Is this column local or syndicated?** _____

**Column Title:** _____

**Name of Columnist:** _____

**Column Topic:** _____

_____

**Is this column local or syndicated?** _____

# Cartoons and Comic Strips

**A cartoon** is a drawing that makes a humorous or satirical comment about some aspect of everyday life—private or public, personal or political. **Comic strips** are groups of cartoons arranged in narrative sequence so that they tell a story or, at least, a small part of a story. While some comic strips deal with current events or political problems, others depict heroic high adventures or the zany antics of a motley crew of animals or other characters.

Find the comic page in your newspaper. Cut out your favorite cartoon or comic strip and paste it in the space below. Then answer the questions at the bottom of this page.

1. What is the name of this cartoon or comic strip? _____

   _____

2. Who writes it? _____

3. Who draws it? _____

4. What is the mood of this cartoon or comic strip? How does it make you feel? _____

   _____

5. What is its message? _____

   _____

   _____

# Sports News

The sports section of a newspaper includes local, regional, national, and international sports news. First, select a news story about a game and paste it below or on the back of this page. Then, answer questions 1–7.

1. What game does this story tell about? _____

2. Who played this game? _____

3. When? _____

4. Where? _____

5. What happened and what was the outcome? _____
   _____

6. Does this story have a dateline? _____ If so, where did it originate?
   _____

7. Does this story have a by-line? _____ If so, who wrote it?
   _____

☆ ☆ ☆ ☆ ☆ ☆ ☆ ☆ ☆ ☆ ☆ ☆ ☆ ☆ ☆ ☆ ☆ ☆ ☆ ☆ ☆

| | |
|---|---|
| **Bonus Box** | Sports columnists often write about important games and the athletes who play in them. Find a column about this game. Compare the style used by the sports reporter with the style used by the sports columnist. Think about the ways in which they are similar and the ways in which they are different. |

# Sports News
## (continued)

Select a sports picture and paste it on this page. Use it to answer questions 8–10.

8. Is this picture an action photograph? _____

9. Which sport is depicted in this photograph? _____

10. Who took the photograph? _____

# The Weather

### Terms to Learn

| | |
|---|---|
| **report** | a detailed account or statement of what has happened in the past |
| **weather report** | an account of what the weather was like at some specified time in the past, often including high and low temperatures, humidity readings, precipitation amounts, and wind speeds |
| **forecast** | an estimate or prediction of what is going to happen in the future |
| **weather forecast** | a prediction of what the weather will be like at some specified time in the future |
| **local forecast** | description of what the weather is expected to be like in your town or city tonight and tomorrow |
| **extended forecast** | description of what the weather is expected to be like over the next few days |

The weather section of a newspaper is very important to many people. For example, your father or mother may use the local forecast to decide what weight of clothing to wear and whether or not to carry an umbrella. Think of five additional reasons someone would want to know the weather forecast. List these reasons on the lines below. Compare your list with the lists compiled by some of your classmates.

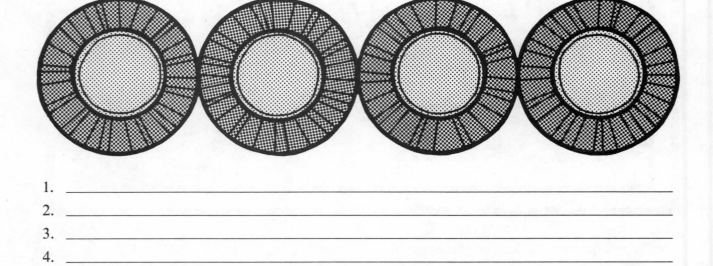

1. _____

2. _____

3. _____

4. _____

5. _____

# The Weather
## (continued)

Find the weather section in your newspaper. Cut it out and paste it on the back of page 36 and on the back of page 37 if you need additional space. Use this section to answer questions 6–14.

6. What is the **weather report** for your area? _____
_____
_____

7. What were the humidity readings? _____

8. Was there any precipitation? _____ If so, how much?
_____ What form did it take? _____

9. At what time did the sun rise today? _____

10. At what time will the sun set today? _____

11. What is the **extended forecast** for your area? _____
_____
_____

12. What was the highest temperature in your state? _____

13. Which city had the highest temperature in the nation? _____

14. List the highs and lows for the following cities:

| | High | Low |
|---|---|---|
| a. Dallas/Fort Worth, Texas | _____ | _____ |
| b. New York, New York | _____ | _____ |
| c. Philadelphia, Pennsylvania | _____ | _____ |
| d. San Francisco, California | _____ | _____ |
| e. San Diego, California | _____ | _____ |
| f. Seattle, Washington | _____ | _____ |

# Advertising

| | |
|---|---|
| **Terms to Learn** | |
| **advertising** | calling something—a candidate, an idea, a product, or a service—to the attention of the public by means of paid announcements in print or broadcast media |
| **ad** | short for advertisement |
| **advertisement** | a paid announcement or public notice printed in a newspaper to call the attention of readers to a candidate, idea, product, or service |

Benjamin Franklin played an important role in the development of newspaper advertising in America. A printer and publisher, he devoted more space in his *Pennsylvania Gazette* to advertising than did any other newspaper publisher of his day. Franklin advertised books, lumber, tea, ships' sailings, and his own invention—the Franklin stove. To improve the appearance of his ads, he used headlines and small illustrations, and arranged them so that they were less crowded than those run by his competitors.

Today, advertising is very important to newspapers. Most of them derive as much as two-thirds of their income from paid advertisements and only about one-third from subscriptions and newsstand purchases.

Do some research to learn the answers to the following questions. Write what you learn on the lines below.

1. What is the price of a single copy of a weekday edition of your newspaper if purchased at a newsstand? _____

2. What is the price of a single copy of the Sunday edition of your newspaper if purchased at a newsstand? _____

3. What is the price of one month's worth of newspapers if purchased this way? _____

4. What is the price of a monthly subscription to your newspaper? _____

5. Does a reader save money by subscribing to the paper rather than purchasing copies individually? _____ If so, how much? _____

# Advertising
## (continued)

Look through your newspaper to find an advertisement that interests you. Cut it out and paste it in the space below. Then use it to answer questions 6–12.

6. Does this ad call the attention of readers to a candidate, an idea, a product, or a service? _____

7. What is it? _____

8. If it is a candidate or idea, what are you supposed to do? _____

_____

9. If it is a product or service, where and when can you get it? _____

_____

10. How much does it cost? _____

11. According to the advertisement, is this price a bargain? _____

12. In addition to the price, what special features or other characteristics make this particular product or service worth considering? _____

_____

# The Insert

<table>
<tr><td colspan="2">Term to Learn</td></tr>
<tr><td>insert</td><td>a separate section of a newspaper which contains advertisements from one company, store, or shopping center, or special information about a single topic, tourist attraction, or upcoming event</td></tr>
</table>

Inserts are often used by stores and shopping centers to advertise sales. Find an insert advertising a sale and use it to answer questions 1–6.

1. Which store or shopping center is having the sale? _____

2. Is this sale occasioned by a season or holiday? _____ If so, which one?

_____

3. On what day does the sale begin? _____

4. On what day does the sale end? _____

5. Are there special store hours during the sale? _____ If so, what are they?

_____

If not, what are the regular store hours? _____

6. List the names or descriptions and the prices of three items that appear to be good buys.

_____  _____

_____  _____

_____  _____

**sale ★ sale ★ sale ★ sale ★ sale**

**SALE SALE SALE SALE SALE SALE SALE**

**SALE ✳ SALE ✳ SALE ✳ SALE**

$ | **Bonus Box** | Check your newspaper each day for a month. On a separate sheet of paper, make a list of the companies, stores, shopping centers, tourist attractions, and special events that are advertised by insert during this period. | $

# Classified Ads

| | |
|---|---|
| **Term to Learn** | |
| **classified ads** | advertisements that appear together in a single section of a newspaper and are organized, or classified, into categories, such as *help wanted, lost and found, for rent,* and *for sale* |

The classified section of a newspaper contains the want ads. These are usually relatively short ads in which individuals describe the items they want to sell, the houses or apartments they want to rent, the jobs they want to find, or the employees they want to hire. People place advertisements in this section because it reaches a large audience, and because the cost is relatively low. The cost is usually based on the number of words or lines used in the ad and on the number of times the ad actually appears in the paper.

Most newspapers provide a contents listing, or index, for the classifed ads section. In some newspapers, this index is called the Classified Guide. Find the index or guide for the classified section of your newspaper and paste it below or on the back of this page.

| | |
|---|---|
| **Bonus Box** | Do some research to learn the cost of placing a classified ad in your newspaper. Record the applicable rates on the back of this page. |

# Classified Ads
## (continued)

1. In which section and on what page do the classified ads begin?

2. Using the classified index or guide, list below six of the major classifications that are used for these ads.

   _____     _____

   _____     _____

   _____     _____

3. Look at the ads themselves. Notice that, for each major classification, there are several subclassifications. For example, if *real estate* is a classification, three related subclassifications might be *commercial property, industrial property,* and *residential income property.* On the lines below, list the subclassifications that are used with one of the major classifications which you listed in response to question 2.

   _____     _____

   _____     _____

   _____     _____

4. Because newspapers often charge by the word or by the line for classified ads, ad writers usually make every effort to eliminate all unnecessary words. The following ad contains nineteen words. Some of them are unnecessary. Pretend that you are an ad writer. On the lines below, rewrite this ad to eliminate the unnecessary words. When you have finished, count and record the total number of words in your shortened version of the ad. How many words did you eliminate?

   > **FOR SALE:** One refrigerator. White with a water dispenser. Only two years old. It will cost $250. Phone 276-0000.

   _____

   _____

   _____

   _____

   Total Number of Words _____

# Special Projects

First, select at least one special project from five of the six skill areas listed below and on page 44. Place a check mark on the line in front of each project you select. Then, follow the project directions carefully.

## Art

_____ 1. Cut a photograph from the newspaper. Fold it in half horizontally or vertically and cut along the fold line. Paste one half of the photograph on a sheet of plain white paper. With a pencil, draw the missing half of the photograph.

_____ 2. Design an ad for something you would like to sell. Write words that will entice people to buy your product. Use marking pens, letter stencils, and a straight edge or ruler to make your ad as neat as possible.

## Health/Science

_____ 3. Divide a piece of paper into five columns. Label these columns **Seeing, Hearing, Smelling, Tasting,** and **Feeling**. Find words in your newspaper that are related to these five senses, cut them out, and paste them in the correct columns. Try to find at least ten words for each column.

_____ 4. Select a news story about some recent scientific discovery or medical advance. On a separate sheet of paper, summarize this story in your own words, paying special attention to the five Ws.

## Math

_____ 5. You have been given $500 to go on a shopping spree. Use newspaper ads to plan your purchases. Cut out pictures of the items you will buy and paste them on a piece of paper. Below each item, write its price. Add all of these prices to determine the total cost of your purchases. Then subtract this total from $500 to see how much change you will have left.

_____ 6. Cut out pictures of ten items that are on sale. Paste them down the left-hand side of a sheet of paper. To the right of these pictures, draw three columns. Label these columns **Regular Price, Sale Price,** and **Savings**. Record the appropriate amounts in each column.

_____ 7. Select two jobs for which wages or salaries are advertised in the classified section of the newspaper. Assuming that there are four forty-hour weeks in each month, figure out the amount that will be paid to employees holding these jobs by the hour, the day, the week, the month, and the year.

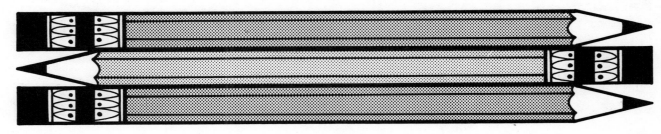

# Special Projects
## (continued)

## Social Studies

_____ 8. Divide a sheet of paper into three columns. Label the columns **City, Country,** and **Continent**. From the datelines in your newspaper, list twenty-five different cities, and record the countries and continents on which they are located.

_____ 9. Divide a sheet of paper into three columns. Label the columns **Person, Job or Position,** and **Importance**. As you read about different people whose names are in the news, fill in the columns with relevant information.

## Vocabulary

_____ 10. Clip letters from headlines in your newspaper to form as many words as you can from the word *newspaper*. Because the word newspaper has two *P*s in it, you may make other words that contain two *P*s, but no proper nouns are allowed.

_____ 11. In your newspaper, find fifteen words that have both a prefix and a suffix. On a separate sheet of paper, list these words, use each one in a sentence, and then underline these words within your sentences.

_____ 12. In the classified section of your newspaper, find twenty-five abbreviations. List these abbreviations on a sheet of paper and write the words for which they stand beside them.

## Writing

_____ 13. Write a letter to the editor expressing your opinion about a current issue or pressing problem. Proofread your letter carefully to be certain that you have said what you intended to say and that you have both spelled the words correctly and used punctuation marks where they are needed.

_____ 14. Write a feature story about a family member or friend whose life, hobbies, and/or special achievements might interest others.

_____ 15. Make an appointment to interview a reporter about being a reporter. Before the interview, think of and list at least ten questions you would like to ask. Remember to include one or more questions about job satisfaction, educational requirements, special training, and necessary or recommended skills.

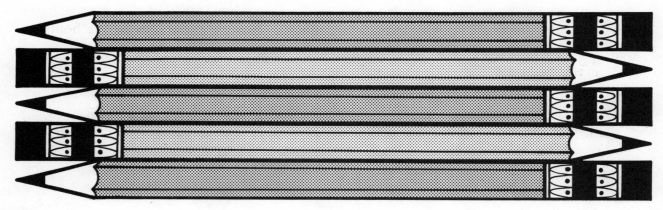

# Glossary

**ad**   short for advertisement

**advertisement**   a paid announcement or public notice printed in a newspaper to call the attention of readers to a candidate, idea, product, or service

**assignment**   a single or continuing story that a reporter is asked to cover for his or her newspaper

**Associated Press (AP)**   a cooperative worldwide news-gathering service

**banked headline**   a headline that contains stacked lines of type of at least two different sizes and/or weights

**banner**   a headline in large type that extends across a newspaper page

**beat**   the place or places a reporter goes or contacts regularly to obtain news, such as school board meetings, the courthouse, or the police department

**by-line**   a line at the top of a newspaper or magazine story, just below the headline, which gives the writer's name

**caption**   a written explanation that appears above or below a photograph or illustration

**classified advertisements**   advertisements that appear together in a single section of a newspaper and are organized, or classified, into categories, such as *help wanted, lost and found, for rent,* and *for sale*

**column**   (1) a narrow, vertical section of printed words on a newspaper page; (2) a newspaper feature that is written regularly by one writer, usually under a by-line

**columnist**   a person who regularly writes an article, or column, for a newspaper

**copy**   typewritten material intended for publication in a newspaper

**cover**   to report news about

**coverage**   the total amount of news reporting done about any one topic or event

**dateline**   the first word or words in a news story giving the place in which the story originated and, occasionally, the date on which it was written

**deadline**   the time after which copy is not accepted for a particular issue or edition of a newspaper

## section of printed words on a ne
## t of news reporting done ab
## HEADLINE IN LARGE TYPE
## which gives the writer's
## places a reporter goes or contacts

# Glossary
## (continued)

**department heads**  the persons responsible for stories written by reporters within various special departments, often including business, government, politics, society, and sports

**edit**  to organize and correct copy so that it conforms to house standards and style; to direct publication of a newspaper

**editor in chief**  employee who heads the newspaper's editorial staff, hires other editors and department heads, directs the writing to reflect the policies and wishes of the newspaper's owners, and writes some editorials

**editorial**  an article expressing the opinion of the newspaper's editor and/or owners on a current issue or topic of interest

**extended forecast** (or **extended outlook**)  description of what the weather is expected to be like over the next few days

**feature stories**  distinctive newspaper articles that are written to inform and/or to entertain

**filler**  a relatively short and unimportant story or a single fact that is used to fill a column

**five Ws**  who, what, when, where, and why—the important information that is usually included in the lead of a well-written news story

**flag** (or **nameplate**)  the name of a newspaper as displayed at the top of the front page

**headline**  words that appear in large, dark type above a newspaper story and tell what the story is about

**illustration**  a drawing used to tell a story or to clarify an idea

**index** (or **departmental index**)  a list of the contents of a newspaper, which is usually found on the front page

**insert**  a separate section of a newspaper which contains advertising from one company, store, or shopping center, or special information about a single topic, tourist attraction, or upcoming event

**international news**  news from the rest of the world (other than your own country)

**kill**  to stop a story from being published

**laserphoto** (or **wirephoto**)  a photograph transmitted by a news-gathering service to member or subscribing newspapers

**lead**  the opening paragraph of a news story, which is usually one sentence and no more than thirty words in length

# photograph transmitted by a new
# policies and wishes of the newspaper's
# SHORT OR UNIMPORTAN
# lly found on the front page
# in large, dark type above a ne

# Glossary
## (continued)

**letters to the editor**   letters written by newspaper readers to the editor of a newspaper to express their opinions about various problems and issues

**local forecast**   description of what the weather is expected to be like in your town or city tonight and tomorrow

**local news**   news from your own town or city

**masthead**   a formal listing of a newspaper's name, owners, officers, points of publication, and subscription and advertising rates, which is usually found on the editorial page

**nameplate** (or **flag**)   the name of a newspaper as displayed at the top of the front page

**national news**   news from the rest of the country (other than your state)

**news editor**   newspaper employee who examines, edits, and approves all news stories submitted by various departments

**obituary**   an official notice of a person's death, often accompanied by an account of his or her life and accomplishments

**picture story**   a single photograph or group of photographs used to tell a story with little or no accompanying text

**regional news**   news from the rest of your state (other than your town or city)

**rewrite**   to revise copy substantially

**standing headline**   a headline that is used regularly to identify a column, feature, or section

**subscription**   an agreement to take and pay for a newspaper that is delivered regularly to a specified address

**syndicated column**   an article or feature that appears regularly in many newspapers across the country

**tip**   a piece of advance or confidential information which is worth investigating further and may become the basis of a news story

**United Press International (UPI)**   a worldwide news-gathering service

**weather forecast**   a prediction of what the weather will be like at some specified time in the future

**weather report**   an account of what the weather was like at some specified time in the past, often including high and low temperatures, humidity readings, precipitation amounts, and wind speeds

OF ADVANCE OR CONFIDENTIAL IN

precipitation amounts, and wi

DISPLAYED AT THE TOP OF THE FR(

VARIOUS PROBLEMS

e in your town or city tonight

# Answer Key

11. a. local
    b. regional
    c. national
    d. international
12. a. who
    b. what
    c. when
    d. where
    e. why

| | |
|---|---|
| 13. H | 22. I |
| 14. J | 23. N |
| 15. L | 24. B |
| 16. E | 25. O |
| 17. D | 26. P |
| 18. G | 27. C |
| 19. K | 28. Q |
| 20. M | 29. R |
| 21. F | 30. A |

**In the Newsroom, Page 27**

| | |
|---|---|
| 1. lead | 4. deadline |
| 2. edit | 5. kill |
| 3. edition | 6. coverage |
| 7. rewrite | |

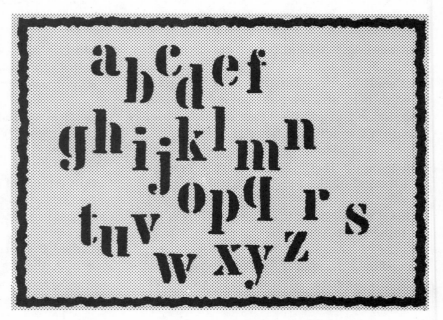

31. a. It is the responsibility of a newspaper to report the news accurately, to distinguish clearly between facts and opinions, to get the facts straight, and—where appropriate—to attribute both facts and opinions to their sources.
    b. This responsibility is important because readers rely on newspapers for accurate information. Inaccurate information can be damaging to individuals and misleading to the general public.
32. a. An editor organizes and corrects copy so that it conforms to house standards and style.
    b. An editor writes editorials.
33. Advertising is an important revenue source for most newspapers because it is relatively stable and because it provides as much as two-thirds of their income. Without advertising, many newspapers would go out of business!
34. The first ten amendments to the U.S. Constitution, which were ratified in 1791 and are known collectively as the Bill of Rights, guarantee freedom of religion, of speech, and of the press to U.S. citizens. Citizens of the Soviet Union are not guaranteed these freedoms.

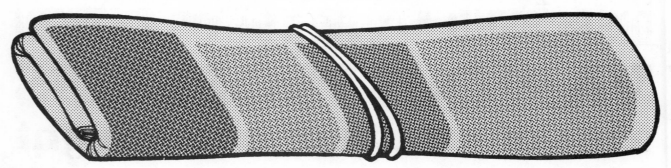